THE WHIMSICAL LIFE OF MAX THE DOG

MAX

a Firehouse Dog

Written by
Allen R. McCaulley

Illustrated by
TANYA PANOVA

Thank you to my wife, Linnea. As always, your
support is needed and critical

Thank you to a group of fifth graders at Rock Island Academy in
Rock Island, Illinois who participated in creating this book. Loi
Kelsi, Stephany, Alyse, Deondre, Kenya, Darius, Noel. Thank you.

Thank you to Dr. Thomas Ryan, principal of Rock Island
Academy, for allowing some of his fifth-grade students to
help with this book. Also, thank you to J.D. Wilson the do-
all technology expert at Rock Island Academy. Dr. Ryan, J.D.
and I hope it was a good experience for the children.

Lou—the project wouldn't have happened without you. I needed
your comments more than ever with this book. Thank you.

Tanya—the fun part for me is seeing what you do with the story.
The words on the page only go so far. You provide the sparkle,
and the magic, that makes the story complete. Thank you.

Gwen—your excellent knowledge of the nuts and bolts of
interior layout make all the difference. Thank you.

Yellow Belly was in the backyard again. He was taking nuts up to his nest.

Then he was dropping them into Max's water bowl. They
made big splashes. He was having great fun.

Max picked up a nut from his water bowl and threw it away. "How can I
keep Yellow Belly from dropping nuts in my water bowl?" wondered Max.

MAX
AX

Max tried to move his water bowl. But it was a stone water bowl, and very heavy. "What can I do?" he thought.

Max growled at Yellow Belly, but Yellow Belly continued
to drop nuts into the water bowl. "What can I do?"

He barked at Yellow Belly, so loud that Max's dad came
out to see what was going on. Then it happened

"Max, dogs can't climb trees," shouted Max's dad. It was too late. Max knew he could, so he did.

"Yellow Belly, STOP dropping nuts into my water bowl!"

Max chased Yellow Belly.

They jumped from the branches of one tree to the next.

Would Max fall from one of the branches?

But then Yellow Belly stopped.

"Max, Old man Moto's house is on fire!"

"We've got to help."

Yellow Belly raced towards the end of a long branch.

Max yelled, "Squirrels can't fly!"

But Yellow Belly knew he could, so he did. He flew through
the air, and through an open upstairs window.

"What can I do to help?" yelled Max. But there
was no reply from inside the house.

Max crawled down the tree as fast as he could.

I have to save old man Moto and his wife!

Max knew what to do.

The fire station was two blocks away, and Max's
friend, Barney, was the firehouse dog.

Max started to run.

"Barney, you've got to help me. Old man Moto's house is on fire. We've got to get your firefighters there. We've got to save the Moto's, and Yellow Belly too."

FIRE DEPARTMENT N.1
OPEN 24h.
CHIEF DOG DOOR

"We'll get the Chief, Max."

ART
CHIEF
WELCOME

Max and Barney pulled Fire Chief Jones out of the firehouse. "Chief Jones, old man Moto's house is on fire. We need your help."

"I've got it Barney. We'll get the guys there immediately."

Did they get there in time?
Max and Barney
couldn't watch.

"Max, Barney, uncover your eyes."
It was Fire Chief Jones. "The Moto's and Yellow
Belly are OK. You saved them and the house!"

Two weeks later there was a day of celebration.

Mayor Mason said, "Max and Barney and Yellow Belly, you are heroes, you saved the Moto's and their house. The entire town loves you, and awards you our citizen of the year medals."